THE
QUI PARLE
PLAY & POEMS

Previous Publications by Kenneth Bernard

Night Club and Other Plays
Two Stories
The Maldive Chronicles (fiction)
How We Danced While We Burned. . . (plays)
Curse of Fool (plays)
The Baboon in the Night Club (poetry)
Clown at Wall (plays, fiction, poetry)
From the District File (fiction)
Ridiculous Theatre, ed. B. Marranca, G. Dasquest
          ("The Magic Show of Dr. Ma-Gico")

THE
QUI PARLE
PLAY & POEMS

Kenneth Bernard

ASYLUM ARTS
PARADISE
1999

Acknowledgments

The author wishes to thank the trustees and Released Time Committe of L.I.U. for grants of time; Stéphane Nahmani (SHOLBY) for his critiques (of everything), his translations, and encouragement; John Vaccaro of the Playhouse of the Ridiculous for his continuing interest; and, again, Elaine Bernard for her long term understanding.

Some of these poems have appeared in *Downtown Brooklyn* and *Poetry New York*.

ISBN: 1-878580-64-7
Library of Congress Catalog Number: 98-74815

Cover collage by Kenneth Bernard.
Book and cover design by Greg Boyd.
Collage photograph by Ed Maietta

Printed by McNaughton & Gunn, Lithographers, Saline, MI.

Asylum Arts
5847 Sawmill Road
Paradise, CA 95969

CONTENTS

For the unknown speaker.

Qui Parle?

(Who Speaks?)

or

The Baby Is Dead:
A Comedy

CAST

Two men and two women (and an optional fifth person), roughly between the ages of 25-50. One set is younger, one older. Their names are variable. Thus they are designated by numbers. They are "characterized" loosely as follows:

#1. Younger female. Represents the weight of history, family, tradition.

#2. Older female. Represents the body, all non-verbal articulations and permutations.

#3. Younger male. Represents chance, randomness.

#4. Older male. Represents the enabling and disabling qualities of the word, language, grammar.

#5. Either sex, any age, any physical condition. At the discretion of the director and actors. If used, this "panelist" is relatively "unconnected" with the others and does nothing other than "field" what may be "neutral" or "problematical" words and phrases. By "field" I mean repeat, but with the widest range of expressiveness (including mal- and non-expressiveness). This can include, for example, questioning, mockery, monotony, satire, levity, and so on. He/she can also repeat words some time after their initial use, as if they have been lingering in his/her consciousness/unconsciousness. His/her English need not be fluent or even existent. Electronic amplification and tricks (e.g. echo, static, dispersed sounds) as desired. It is also possible to have this person present but do absolutely nothing. His/her use will only be suggested in the text as one possibility. Much will depend on the actor's perceptions of what he/she is hearing, the particular rhythms, conflicts, etc. of particular evenings, and so on. It is desirable, if only to promote some alleviating "coherence," that his/her enunciations during the play progress in the direction of greater urgency and emphasis.

The four main characters, however, are not rigidly enclosed in their descriptions. They cross over at times. There are also suggestions (spoken and unspoken) of personal relationships, outside the arena of the "play" they are performing, but these are never specific enough to build coherent structures on. They also change. It is important that the actors discover and use whatever relationships they discover to exist within their lines. It is expected that some of these will develop and some will change from performance to performance. They should all be physically agile, but #2 in particular should be especially skilled, perhaps with dance training. They should all also have at least rudimentary musical skills, for they will be required to play on toy or made-up instruments, noise-makers, etc. They should have extreme flexibility in terms of "character" and be able to suspend normal psychology and motivation as much as possible in their acting, working more from rhetoric and picking up what they need as they go along. Whenever a given name appears in the text, they may change it as they wish. They may also appropriate each other's lines if during the rehearsal period they feel a particular affinity for some others as a result of personal association or the group's interrelationship. Occasionally, as the run continues, this might happen spontaneously, at a particular performance, requiring sudden adjustments all around. Intelligence, a very keen ear, total attentiveness, and a sense of music, "noise," and rhythm necessary. The length of certain sections will depend on their own mood and interaction from performance to performance. They should be able to imitate the sounds and movements of animals, particularly birds, and be willing to explore sub-lingual human sounds. They may use a particular refrain at will to each other, the audience, or no one in particular, consisting of the following or some variation: "Tell me your real name." "Will you tell me your name?" "Can you tell me your real name?" When used, it is always ignored. The text, again, will only suggest a few possible occasions for its use.

The stage is set with a low table, behind which at least four actors on chairs (of their own choosing). On the table, the toy and make-shift instruments they will use, perhaps some of the props. Whatever else they will need can be off to the side, under the table, etc. Whenever they come out from the table, they may choose how to do it, e.g. under, over, around. Moderate to severe whiteface with make-up. Wigs probably useful: otherwise, hair stylized. Dress: elegant but faded, perhaps slightly tattered. The lights come up on them slowly. From the audience view they are seated, left to right, as follows:

#1,2,3,4. This, however, may be changed. #5, if present, may be anywhere. A long pause before they begin.

#1: *[Rising]* Who is it that speaks? Not I. Not I. Certainly not I, said the little brown bear, the pink pigeon, the ochre otter. Not I, but my grandmother speaks. Not she, but her aunt. Not she, but the rocky village by a sea where she was so unhappy. Not it, but the year 1804 and everything that happened to it, then and there. Speaks, but never fully. Gives voice to what has no voice, is bigger than voice, is other than voice, speaks nevertheless, imperfectly, undecipherably, incoherently, speaks, speaks, speaks, who, who, who, what, what speaks, -eaks, -eaks, -k, -k, -k, -k, -k, -s, -s, -s, -s. *[SHE sits abruptly]*

#2: *[Rising, articulating movements and expressions as she speaks, with help from the others]* —My voice is movement. If you can see it, then you hear me. What is the word pain when you hear it? Nothing. A coat without a body in it. But if I scream? If I gasp, if I moan, and as I do these things I move.... Thus. Thus and thus. You can give it the word pain. You can say that is pain. Yes. I see pain. I can feel her pain. That angle is such and such a pain. That thrust, coupled with that moan or groan, or utterance, or cry, or gasp, or breath is pain. But what pain? What pain is that? In my life I shall have two million, four hundred thousand and sixty-two pains, not all of them visible.

ANYONE: Do tell us your name.

#2: One will kill me. One will be a sequence with a dozen others scattered over twenty years and will settle in a chamber of my heart. Which one do you see and to what degree? How do you name it? Do you dare to name it? Do you dare to call it my higgledy-piggledy pain?

#5: Higledy-piggledy.

#2: —Several thousand will be here. *[She puts her hand on her crotch]* Oh, yes. Here. One of them will be something like this. This movement, this sound. Can you name it, call it, communicate it? Pain number 3,265? *[She laughs]* —It is still my pain. It is always my pain. Even if you do not speak it, leave it whole, it is my pain. Silence helps but does not make it yours. Feel it, imitate it, write music for it, hold me, love me, kill me—it is still and forever my pain. And your pain is your pain. And our words and our movements and your pain and my pain flutter like cumbersome birds colliding in the night. The earth is filled with the putrefaction of their decaying bodies. They fall and they rot. And here we perform ceremonies. We are a community in the service of something. Look. Watch. Still your deceiving mind. This movement is a ceremony. This sound is a ceremony. Together they are a ceremony for a bird with a large head and a small body. Its claws clutch at nothing. It is falling. It has been struck. And as it falls it emits unholy squawk, which becomes the song that ends this particular part of the ceremony.

> *[She ceases her movement abruptly, holds the position briefly, then chants, nasally and atonally, meaningless sounds. She stops abruptly, curtsies prettily and returns to her place, as #3 rises and empties one of his pockets on the table]*

#3: I am this miscellany and all miscellanies. Me and my dog. The angel and I. Pablo, the great divide, and *mutatis mutandis*. Great holy brethren and the dinner gong, the dingy gong, the dinghy gong. *[pause]* The gong-gong. The gong-along. The gong-gong-gong-gong!

> *[He scoops up the objects and drops them on the table like dice several times]*

I am grateful for this flat and level surface. Were the floor askew, the walls awry, my fate would, like this table, be different. Thus does a life go. I could of course then prop up a leg or two and make the table true, calling this piece of wood or whatever Plato or my dog Harry or the sixth rule of benevolent conduct.

#5: Dog Harry.

ANYONE: But what is his real name?

#3: —This pen is inkless, but I carry it near my heart. Found in a gutter on a cold February morning, it was my only free thing in a long winter, and I write all my secrets with it, secrets even to me. Every book ever written has another book between the lines, written with an inkless pen, on which there are true but unreadable commentaries. And between its lines, another book. If you would count, you would see there eighty-seven cents. That is almost a history of my life. Certainly as good as any other. It is the result of four transactions over two and a half days. In one of them I bought four cucumbers and a turnip and thought of my paternal grandmother, who had a severe moustache.

#5: Moustache.

#3: In another I bought a particular newspaper. In another the token I needed to travel. And in a fourth, a worthless item to gratify my vanity. I could talk days about my vanity, days about my concern for odor and its inexplicable connection with dank cellars where I chopped wood in dim light while a silent uncle with a bald head always under a hat watched. Oh, how you would begin to know me.

ANYONE: Won't you tell us your real name?

#3: But knowing me, what would you know? What would it mean? The thousand facts—fact? *facts?*—would be like a thousand birds scattering in a thousand directions and to call it me, to say it I—*I, I, I, I*—would be courage, risk, lunacy, and practical enough, but worthless and of offensive odor. I forego the cucumbers, etc. for now, but want that you note *[Pointing]* the button, the dirty cleenex—oh, those keys *[Pause]*—the bobby pin, and the rubber band. Glorious, glorious and maddening miscellany. How you would love me—were I to talk about them.
    [He sits abruptly]

#4: *[Rising]* That leaves me.

ANYONE: Name, please?

#4: To be accounted for. *I am my words.* Without them I might not exist. They formulate me. They contour me. I am their work of art. *[Deliberately]* I am their work of art. —What a work of art is man? ... Satisfactory. B+. I am a creature with a soul? I do not live by bread alone? ... Satisfactory, satisfactory, satisfactory.

#5: B+.

#4: —*Not* satisfactory! Hell and damnation, *not satisfactory*! But can you do better? Now these birds that have scattered in a thousand directions—if each they had a different song?
> *[The others imitate bird sounds, singly and slowly at first, then enjambed and more quickly, the volume increasing, moving vaguely into intonation]*

Stop!
> *[Silence]*

And if one, less fit perhaps on erratic journey, feet somehow bloodied—
> *[#2 moves awkwardly forward, settles into a grotesque position, showing a bloodied foot, and lets out an unholy bird squawk]*

—what then? What then?

#5: What then? What then?
> *[The others resume their calls, more quietly, as counterpoint to #2's squawks]*

#4: Stop! —Back to the words. The words. Take "stop," even. What, ever, stops? We may say everything stops. Or nothing stops. But if *something*, some one thing only, stops, there you have the measure of a goosebump on my arm, a lump in my throat, a cut to civilization's heart. There you are beginning to see *me*. Oh, warty me! Stop! Stop, stop, and stop! Can you thrill to it as I do? I say stop, and worlds crumble. And on their ruins I build anew. Stop. I erect my organ. Stop. I splatter you all. Stop. Stop, stop. But if you take my stop, take it away, I begin to disappear. I disintegrate, my arm falls, off. Because I am my words. And my words are my world. And you are my words, even if you do not understand them, even unformulated. *Stop!* *[He laughs]* And your words are my words—

#1: *Stop! [She laughs]* Only up, I, to a, think, point, Jimmy. —And by the way, you didn't erect much last night. —Oh, warty, warty night!

#3: Stop!

#2: Stop!
   [They laugh]

#1: If I could only tell you about my Aunt Edna. Really great Aunt Edna, grandmother's younger sister.

#2: Stop?

#1: No. No stop. Which is still stop nevertheless. And I go on. —Will you be Aunt Edna?

#2: The one that loved you truly?

#1: The one that saved me for myself, for life. I was an ugly girl for so many reasons.

ANYONE: Tell us your real name, won't you?

#5: Warty! Higgledy-piggledy! Dog Harry!

#4: Reasons? Word, word, word. By a river you never knew you would not have been ugly. Frog-eyed and pouty-lipped, you would have been loved as wet spirit of the water.

#3: Stop! *[He laughs]* Exhilarating. I await and watch the wet spirit of the water, frog-eyed, pouty-lipped, and loved.

#2: May I move like Aunt Edna, talk like Aunt Edna?

#1: Please. You may *be* Aunt Edna.
   [#2 assumes the role of an elderly Aunt Edna, moves slowly front. During this exchange, #3 and #4 interject bird sounds]

#2: Come here, you ugly little child.

#1: Is ugly just another word?

#1: Yes. Ugly is as pretty does. I see in your bones my own mother's back, broken through forty years of desire on top of mindless work.

#1: Rugs?

#2: Yes. Eight hours and more each night she held her hands over her head pulling yarns. And on her breaks stole spools to give to sicker friends to make rugs for pennies for such as you. Did you know the rugs you played on were *crocheted* by old ladies whirling on low stools with twisty fingers like grim fate?

#1: I loved those rugs, prickly though they were.

#2: Yes, prickly. No soft comforts there.

#1: And that prickly—

#2: Yes, that prickly, from the night shifts and tired arms and the sick old ladies, is in your bones—

#1: *Bones*? Another word?

#2: Bone*head*, if you wish, calcic fiber of your being. Somewhere resides in you that dreary plant with floating fibers sucked into a thousand lady lungs to produce—

#1: But—

#2: Yes. I know. They never lived long enough to really cough alarmingly.

#1: But I did hear your mother cough. Was it really *your* mother? I was only five, but I remember clearly how it cracked the clear cold nights like a rifle's bullet. I used to wonder, did it hurt her throat? Why didn't anyone complain at being woken? Somehow, at breakfast it was never mentioned. The fire and corn muffin smells dissipated night troubles.

#2: Woken, child? Mentioned? Woken was nothing. Her life was racing to another end than coughing would have brought her. Do you remember when she doubled over?

#1: Yes, I think I do ... remember. Sometimes when she, someone, held me she sometimes leaned, crushed me in her lap as if she had been kicked in the back.

#2: Yes, exactly. But never a sound, one death supplanting another. Did it really matter, after a certain point?

#1: No, never a sound. I'd hear her breathe hard, and then she'd kiss me, and sometimes I'd feel a drop, a tear—

#2: Oh, yes, she could cry. She knew what to cry about, though never often.

#1: What kisses they were. It wasn't only pain.

#2: No. The tears were more than that. Something was going.

#1: It wasn't only life.

#2: No. There was a whole beauty—pain and all.

#1: Oh, how she loved me, *loved* me!

#2: Loved you, and loved the life still growing in you.

#1: As—

#2: Death was growing monstrously in her.

#1: I don't remember when she died. Does death have to grow monstrously?

#2: You were there. You even held her hand unthinkingly, playing with her twisted fingers.

#5: Higgledy-piggledy. Higgledy-piggledy.

#1: But I knew.

#2: Yes. You knew.

#1: And now I don't. Her fingers went stiff. The blood in them dried.

#2: It doesn't matter. It's all in your bones.

#1: *[Feeling herself]* There's so much in my bones. —And in *your* bones, too. —Aunt Edna?

#2: Yes? What is it, my child?

#1: Are ... Are you dying, too?
       [Pause. They slowly approach and embrace]

#2: Yes. I'm dying. And that, too, is in your bones.
       [Pause. The bird calls are very soft. They resume their places]

ANYONE: Dare we ask their real names?

#3: Sometimes the dice are called the bones. Give the bones a shake and toss. Last Tuesday morning—what a comfort Tuesday is—for no reason I could tell, my back was sore and I therefore tied my left shoe badly. Waiting for the train I tripped on an undone lace and pushed a young woman so that she knocked a post with her elbow. Her left elbow, if you like. No great damage, but I could see it hurt. Silently she cursed, her lips barely moving. Encephalitic parasite! Fat-toe! Pismiric excrescence! It broke her train of thought. A jagged edge in the contour of her day. I could see she felt it just one of those innumerable unplanned, unexpected things that make up most of our days without our usually noting them. On the train she looked at me once or twice—I was waiting—no expression, shutting me out. What could she say, after all? What could anyone say? And yet—

#1: Did you tie your shoe?

ANYONE: What was her name?

#3: I don't remember. I must have. When I got to work, it was tied. But when she looked at me, I don't know whether it was tied or not. Something lost there. What? Why?

#5: Fat-toe.

#2: She probably thought, "Why the hell don't you tie your flanken shoe?"

#3: *Flanken?*

#4: Word.

#2: In a manner of speaking.

#3: I thought of her the entire day.

#1: —But you might have married her. You might—

#3: Yes. I thought of that. All of that. We don't notice. We don't notice. She—she was pretty. One sees pretty, pretty people all one's life—once.

#2: Does it ever occur to you that your shoes are just filled with so much meat?

#3: I could never dance if I thought that.

#2: I could.

#4: Meat-in-the-shoe dance. Fat-toe-meat dance.

#2: Yes. Something like that.

#1: But your back–why was it sore? That's important.

#3: Too complicated. And a mystery, to boot. Unrecognized, of course. — And back to foot, no?

#2: Foot one.

#5: To boot.

#4: Did you ever see her again?

#2: Back, foot, elbow, glare, love, marriage, boot—

#3: I'm already married, as you well know.

ANYONE: Then tell us your real name.

#3: —And anyway, I wanted to talk about something else from my pocket.

#1: What?

#3: The button.

#2: Wouldn't you like the meat-in-the-foot dance first?

#3: We should all like a meat-in-the-foot dance first.

#4: Primary and essential. —Because I say so.
     [#2 rises. The others take out instruments]

#2: Yes, music. Always music. Some kind of music. Even if we don't hear it.
Even if it—

#4: Meat-in-the-ear music.
     *[As they play, in no particular harmony, rhythm, or melody, #2
     dances a meat-in-the-shoe dance, emitting sounds, sobs, laughs, etc. at
     intervals. One or more of the others may sing snatches of wordless song.
     The duration may vary, e.g. wane, pause, pick up again. The actors
     decide when they are done. #2 returns to her place at the table]*

#2: *[Staring, articulating slowly]* Qui parle? Qui parle? Qui parle?

ALL: *[Enjambed, softly]* Qui parle? Qui parle? Who speaks? Qui parle? Who
speaks? ...
     [Silence]

#5: Higgledy-piggledy. Dog Harry.

#3: The button—a speech.

OTHERS: Ahem, ahem, ahem. . . . .

#3: All speeches are equally wonderful.

#1: But first a digression.

#3: All digressions are equally wonderful.

#1: Yes.

#3: May I call you . . . Helen?

#1: Yes.

#3: May I call you Mary?

#1: Yes.

#3: May I call you . . . Anastasia?

#1: Yes.

#3: Beatrice?

#1: Yes.

#3: Clorinda?

#1: Yes. Yes.

#3: Clara? Ingrid? Cucamunga?

#5: Cucamunga.

#1: Yes. A thousand times, yes. And also Margaret, Iolanthe, Dirigible, Judith, Wee Mousie, and T-Bone.

#3: You have a thousand names.

#1: Yes. All meaningless.

#3: Then who are you? What is your true name?

#1: I am Judith out of Harry and Lydia, who were out of Adolf and Eugenia and Benito and Nanette, and so, so, so on—that very Judith. Who broke her leg when she was three. That Judith. Who lost all her wisdom teeth in one year when she was eighteen. That Judith. Whose tonsils were 3.526 centimeters thick before she had them out in a botched operation that left her with a sensitive throat, left her a bad singer, left her with peculiar thoughts about her body, doctors, fate. *That* Judith. And so, so, so, so and on and on.

#3: I see. It's the *so* and the *on* that matter, isn't it?

#1: What? Am I hearing what I'm hearing?

#3: I mean I see that I should really call you Judith-olana-buraka-milazzi de pakka—that is to say *that* Judith.

#1: Closer and closer. Except that I prefer the name Helen and go by the name Mary.

#3: We can manage.

#1: Manage what?

#3: Why . . . when I hold you . . . thus . . . I can say—

#1: Dear, dear Judith-olana-buraka-milazzi de pakka . . . how I do love you.

#3: Yes. That is exactly right. And you can say—

#1: Oh, George-gabooli-tempaca-strungena . . . you give me the shakes and the willies.

#3: The Williams, please. I give you the Williams. —Am I really that George? —And then we kiss?

#1: And then we kiss.
    [They kiss]

#3: And then we scream?

#1: And then we scream.
    [They scream]

#3: And then we cry?

#1: And then we cry.
    [They cry]

#3: Oh, Mary-Helen-Judith-lapogonda-miloni de calbroko-caca-buku-sussi-la mroch . . . will I come to know your flesh as I am coming to know your soul, to know you, the real, real, really and only you?

#5: Mroch. MROCH! Cucamunga!

#1: *[Holding him at arm's length]* It's a real question, a genuine problem, a praxis devoutly to be desired, an impossibility given certain problems of time, perception and so on—but, well, maybe, umm, we're only human, who knows, we'll see, wipe your mouth.

#3: I'll wait with bated breath.

#1: And then you'll die.
    [Pause. They stare at each other. #1 sits]

#3: Thank you.

ANYONE: Do they have names?

#3: Once there was a button.

OTHERS: No, no, no, no. . . .

#3: Once upon a time?

#4: Definitely no.

#3: When the button found itself cornered, death staring it in the face—
[He looks around for approval] the button began to dance. Yes, dance for its
very life. The very button from my raincoat with the removable lining, which
someone here—unnamed—bought me for my b-b-b-birthday, out of love,
love for this very me, did I feel it, did I deserve it, was I even there, even
though I wore the coat at once?

#2: Don't look at me.

#1: Nor me. I can love a nobody as well as a somebody, but this is not the
place to reveal anything.

#4: Stick with button. Was there lint on it. Chocolate? Any unspecified
substance like gelsemium or gelignite? A trace of epigynum?

#3: Yes. Fourteen days in the same pocket. The possibilities were rife. —
Which reminds me of something.

#4: Vague echo of past glory? Faded transcendence? Progression? Constipa-
tion?

#3: Yes. Something like that. Something bracing. At any rate, it popped off
in the street—which one I don't know, why, I don't know. Something like
my back, I suppose. Breathed in too handsomely, twisted maybe—why? why
did I twist?—a pretty girl?—a dog relieving or reliving itself—like us humans—humans?—come here, dog-dog, and I'll love you for your dogginess—
oh, for a human bone to chew on.

#5: Dog-dog. —MROCH! Dog Harry!

#3: The relationship that went into that coat-giving—the looks, the lust, the tears and years, the shared and sheared moments of life whizzing by with a million micro-encrustations—well, I won't go into that. It's too complicated. Cosmic loss. She's here, but I don't know who she is right now. Our every encounter is a painful formality in a new ritual. Every step is fraught.

#4: Word. Word. I hear another one. Like rain drops.

#3: You mean . . . ought I say fraught: Or nought fraught? *[He laughs]*

#1 and #2: Droll. Droll. How very drolly.

#4: Fraught and drolly. What an embarrassment of riches. What a bare ass of riches. What a bare ass of Richard. The fraught and droll corpus rises. And—

ANYONE: What is his real name?

#5: MROCH! . . . Cucamunga. . . . Fat-toe.

#3: Well—

#1: Be that as it may—

#2: Yes, do finish.

#3: In those fourteen days I had come to finger the little button. *[He thinks a moment]* —Yes, yes, I admit it—finger the little button in ways I had never imagined, wouldn't confess, even under penalty of blood-letting. It wasn't, you see, really a button any more, but. . . .

#1: A talisman?

#3: A what?

#1: A talis—

#3: Don't say it.

#2: *Stop?*

#4: Oh, dear. Not another dance. I hope. Not.

#2: No. No talismanic dance.

#3: What about—*talismania?*
      [They look at each other, happily expectant and alert to the possi-bilities. They bring up their instruments and play. #2 dances a taismania. Quick, frenetic. She laughs throughout. #4 joins her. Per-cussion. Abrupt finish and pose]

#4: My goodness. Almost a tableau.

#1: Giving up words, Harry?

#4: *[Returning]* Never. Let *me* finish off button.

#3: Good. I need a rest. And I've done only one pocket. Not to mention drawers, bags, boxes, trunks, barrels, canisters, and secret compartments.

#1: Squeeze a lot of body in a barrel. But compartments are different.

#4: Well, there was button, brick walls on three sides, very marginal types advancing on fourth, no fifth in sight, knives drawn, pistols drawn, long teeth, salivating yellow pus, bloodshot eyes, jagged ears—button was their dream of a victim—

#1: And victim of a dream. Only his shiny virtues to protect him.

#4: Right. And what virtues they were.

#1: Probity, dignity, consistency, thrift, respect for law, a proper sense of history, cultural loyalty, and utter reverence for tadpoles.

#5: Yellow pus. Mroch.

#4: Step by step they advanced on this paragon of a button. Then they slithered and oozed. The space was filled with them. The air—

#1: Was thick.

#4: Button thought—

#1: Of his mother.

#4: Perhaps.

#1: His true love?

#4: Too young.

#2: Who, then?

#4: He could smell every foul breath. There was no way out, no help, no secret weapon or strategy, no prayer. His throat constricted. The knives flashed, the teeth gleamed, the pistols cocked—

#3: *Cocked?* The pistols *cocked?* Now there's one even I could dance.

#1: Did they get him?

#3: Well, no. You see, he was a she. At the final moment—Button lifted his skirt.

#1: His skirt?

#3: Yes. Lifted his skirt and—

#1: Yes?

#3: *Split in two.* There you have it. Broken button. Confusion. End of drama. Skirt down. New Beginning. New Beginning.

#1: She was saved?

#3: Well, not exactly.

ANYONE: What was her name?

#4: Acceptable. Quite acceptable.

#1: I knew it all the time. What a comfort an end is.

#4: I couldn't live without an end.

#2: If I may, I would like to articulate further the "not exactly."

#4: You mean I've missed a word or two?

#2: I might need help.

#1: *[Mock-yelling]* Help!

#2: *[Rising, an announcement]* A medley of common, that is, universal gestures, with select exceptions in interpretation, followed by some not so common ones, more or less totally open to interpretation. In other words—

OTHERS: Not exactly!

#1: Ta-daaa!

#2: You've got it.

#4: Right up the nose.

#3: Now everyone watch carefully. Or uncarefully, for that matter.

> *[#2 extends her left arm slowly, places the side of her right hand at the elbow joint, then makes a fist with the left hand and raises it to a right angle as she mouths "Fuck you" and stares at the audience. Pause]*

Behold the classic fungoo. Ancient order of the dragon.

#1: *[Rising energetically, placing both thumbs in her sides, arms akimbo, mugging]* The chop-suey! *[Sits]*

#5: Fungoofungoofungoofungoofungoofun—

#2: Variations.
>   *[Same as first gesture but palm outward]*

#4: Clearly, this says, "Stop or I fuck you up the ass."

#1: "No, I will not be violated. Tonight. Tonight is inviolate. Hearken ye to other occasions."

#5: Fungoo.
>   *[#2 performs the same gesture, index finger up]*

#4: "Pay attention or I—"

#5: Fungoo.

#4: Etcetera. Facial optional.

#3: *[Still interpreting]* "Just one moment, sir or madam. I take strong exception to what you say. But implicit in my reservation is that I shit on you anyway."
>   *[Same gesture by #2, thumb extended and slowly brought into her mouth as far as it will go. She sucks it in and out. Silence at the table. #1 looks to #3 and #4 for commentary]*

#1: Well?

#5: Fungoo.

#4: A bit more difficult. Would you do it again?

#3: With more expressive detail maybe?
>   *[#2 does so, noisily]*
"I fuck you by fucking myself?"

#4: No, it's more like . . . "I'm fucking you if you don't fuck me."

#1: *[Imitating #2]* I like it. It reminds of of–

#3: You've got plenty of movement but none of the feeling.

#1: And you do?

ANYONE: Does she have a name at this point?

#4: The eyes are important, I think. For example, if you are at a social gathering, you see someone you like, perform the gesture, but your eyes are closed, it would be entirely solipsistic, a wet dream, something like masturbating in a closet or a crowd. But if your eyes are open—

#3: Eyebrows popping up and down—

#4: Yes. Then there's some sort of engagement, confrontation, contact.

#1: She might do it back.

#4: Yes. And them, who knows?
    [#1 tries it on #3, eyebrows popping. He does it back with a firm look]

#1: But you're sneering. I can feel it. I never felt so embarrassed.

#4: *[To #2]* Jane?
        [#2 breaks her pose]
What do you call it?

#2: I-am-lighter-than-feathers-when-you-salivate.

#4: Quaint. Stupid of us not to see it immediately.

#3: Are there any other variations?
    [#2 performs the same gesture, middle finger extended upward]

#4: Obviously for emphasis.

#1: Why is there never any question where *that* finger goes? Why not a nostril?

#4: That's the pinky.

#5: Pinky pinky pinky pinky.

#3: First, obviously it has to be *up* something. And there are only a limited number of things it could be up.

#1: Then it's sexist.

#3: Sexist?

#1: Well, it obviously could never be up your penis. Women have an extra *up*.

#4: Oh, come. The aperture is clear. And non-discriminatory. Analyze, my dear.

#1: Then tell me this. I'll go along with the a-hole. But is it from in front or behind? Grant me that.

#3: Now there we have some possibility of cultural difference.

#4: I'd say it depends on whether the recipient is advancing or retreating.

#1: From? Toward? What is the *thing*?

ANYONE: And what is its name?

#2: *[Breaking her pose]* But in fact, since it's only a gesture, nobody is ever actually invaded. It's all good clean fun.

#4: *Invaded*?

#3: Good god, another word.

#1: Stop!

#4: And handsome, too.

#2: The gesture lives in a different space.

#1: You mean nobody is ever fucked who is fucked?

#4: Only a very limited number. Who can say what "fucked" truly is?

#3: Let's get to some of those not so common gestures.

#1: I still haven't gotten anywhere with the common ones.

#3: Well . . . how about one more common and then . . .

[#2 grasps her crotch, thrusts her pelvis forward several times, and licks the thumb of her other hand. Long pause]

#1: She's testing for the weather.
    [#3 and #4 laugh]

#3: No, no, Alice.

#1: I'm Alice?

#3: It's weather only if it's the forefinger and then held up facing away from the body. Into the wind, you see.
    [#2 performs the same gesture several times but now wetting her forefinger and holding it into the wind]

#1: *Now* she wants to know the weather?

#4: Well, say the atmosphere or climate. Haven't you watched television lately? The maps especially? What's moving in and out, up and down, and how fast? Tremendous expectation, and their mouths are always wet from sucking someone off.

#1: I don't really like this one. Do another, please-please-please, Jane?
       [#2 turns away from the audience, grasps one buttock firmly, lifts, and thrusts a fist forward twice. The others make flatulating noises and laugh]

#4: Well, no question there, is there?

#3: Put it into words.

#1: Not "Fuck you" again. I'm getting very confused.

#4: Let me give you some possibilities. Do it once more, please, Janie.
       [#2 does, with same effects]
Okay. Number one—"Not on your life, Buster." Number two—

#3: "Eat it."

#4: Well, no. I was going to say—"That was the pits."

#1: Then it doesn't have to be personal. I mean, it can be directed at a thing. An event, maybe. Just the thing for a body in deliberation.

#3: Yes. Some people leaving here later—or now—might try it, for example. discreetly, of course. Can it be done discreetly, Jane?
       [#2 does it discreetly, with discreet accompanying sounds]
Wonderful. One, two, three—discreet gesture. Cocktails at four. Civilization is so grand. Meet me at the epicenter.

#1: Well, it's no Che Guevara, that's for sure.

#4: I want to note that this very same gesture in innermost Borneo still commonly means, "I am constipated. Can you help me, poke me maybe?"

ANYONE: Oh, dear, what would his name be?
       [#2 demonstrates as #4 continues]

#4: A person so afflicted will walk around the village or river bank—pay attention to that river bank—like a lost tortured soul, grasping and lifting *her* buttock, thrusting *her* fist, making froglike croaks, and hoping someone will have a spare charm or remedy to relieve her condition. The problem is that sometimes there are village people of newer orientations who walk around with the aforementioned intentions to their gestures, i.e. fuck you, baby.

    [#1 simulates one of newer orientation, with #3 providing sound effects]

When these two cross each other's path, a very serious confusion can be the result. Sometimes a smouldering frustration or anxiety can threaten to erupt into violence. But—

    [#1 and #2 glare at each other, each holding her buttock, etc. They break their poses abruptly. #1 retreats to her seat]

#2: I'm glad you brought up Borneo, because in nearby New Guinea there is a wonderful gesture that I hope will find its way into the West.

#3: And what is that, pray tell?

#2: Well, there it is called the "Bukkavinda maakee." It's done thus. *[Demonstrating as she talks]* One swings one's arm up abruptly. Then one jabs one's thumb into the armpit several times, maintaining either a kind of sneer or a simpering look on one's face, depending on one's sex and age.

#1: And what does it mean?

#2: Well, of course translation is always dangerous, but, loosely speaking—and shouldn't we always be loosely speaking?—it means "That was one lousy meal." Used on certain semi-formal occasions only. For example, your prospective in-laws have invited you to a meal. However, they do not think you are quite good enough for their child. Your fingernails are not long enough. You do not squeeze your sounds out properly. In some parts of the world, speech is proper only when it emerges like constipated turds. If it's not one thing it's another. The meal reflects all this. You bide your time, eat the meal with good humor and so on, and only at the last possible moment, as you leave, do you fling up your arm and poke your thumb. It is considered a great humiliation, a kind of perfect *turning of the tables*—

#1: Word!

#3: Stop!

#2: And here's the kicker. The one who thumbs his armpit must then run like hell and hide for three days, because it is a quite excusable reaction to kill him for such an insult. All the relatives of both sides are brought into an elaborate game of hide and seek and seem to enjoy it as if it were a carnival although it could turn out quite bloody.

#3: And after three days?

#2: He is safe. The insult is incorporated as an official part of community history and is thereafter sacrosanct.

#4: Rather good here, in restaurants, I would think.

#2: Well, it's difficult to say how we might use it. For one thing, you see, it's so much more effective there because of the nudity. The armpit is really revealed—sweat, hair, smell, goosebumps, ceremonial scars, folds and creases, paint, bugs. But here—

#3: A lot of split seams!

#2: Yes.

#1: Taxis stopping! Strangers saying hello! And no follow-through like, "In the year that Leon of Anna and Ludovico insulted the family of Cleo and lived. . . ."

#2: Yes. Like dropping it off a cliff.

#3: But it could be more suave, you know, have more style. [Demonstrating as he speaks] A kind of slow floating upward movement of the arm and a mild tapping of a finger instead of a thumb. Something like tapping the nose in Albania as an all-purpose response to a weather query.

#4: And what would it mean?

#3: Well, I should day something like, "Thank you so much. I'd *love* to come again.

#1: But no sneer.

#3: Oh, no no. At most a kind of sweet simpering look, perhaps a sniff.

#4: Or an invitation to sniff.

#3: *Yes.* Yes, indeed. Complete trust is the ticket. To smell someone's armpit, or to be invited thereto, impinges on the realm of trust. Clearly. Local bankers. Psychotherapists.

#4: And intimacy.

#3: Yes. Quite a turn-about from New Guinea.

#4: Well, other side of the world, you know.

#3: Topsy-turvy. Dipsy-doodle. Other side of the coin.
        [Demonstrating, offering #1 his armpit to sniff. #1 pauses, then raises her fist, elevates her middle finger, and slowly puts it in her nostril, remaining expressionless]
Monumental.
        [#2 and #4 take out instruments for a brief cacophonous interlude. Pause]

#3: —Now about that eight-seven cents.

ANYONE: I hope he's finally going to tell us his real name.

#5: Dipsy– Dipsy—

#1: I was wondering when we were going to get to it.

#5: *Dipsy*—

#1: If I were to break my piggy bank there's no telling what I'd say.

#2: I'll say.

#1: And just what does that mean, Hannah?

#2: It mean [sic], honey, your piggy bank is very large.

#3: You say that, Marilyn, as if—as if it were very—very fraught—

#4: *Stop right there.* It is sufficient. Yes, it is very fraught. Her large piggy bank is very fraught.

#1: You can't stop there.

#3: We did. We do. *I'm* speaking. Do a gesture, if you like.
     [She does or does not]
—I started out with ten dollars. When I reached a certain age, my mother told me never to start out with anything less than ten dollars.

#2: And your father?

#3: Wasn't in the picture then.

#4: Oh, dear. What picture are we talking about? Then.

#3: Let me give you the most relevant detail first. All my life I've hated zucchini. Don't know why. Until three years ago. And then suddenly I was mad for it. Thought my health required zucchini. All my cells shifted. Ate it every week. A kind of memorial to my mother, I thought.

#1: It *is* good for you.

#5: Dipsy-doodle. Mroch.

#3: So it is. And indubitably. Well, anyway—it's always anyway, isn't it?—I was doing my weekly zucchini stint—

#4: Where?

#5: Stint. —Doodle. Piggy-doodle. Pig-doodle.

#3: Buddy's Market, if you must know, Richard. Korean. But good English and never cheats. It's a big joke with everyone. You come in and say, "Hi, Buddy!" and he gives you this big Korean laugh and says "I Kwong." Only half the time he's not really laughing. I think he might actually hate us.

#5: Big Korean laugh.

#1: Well, why doesn't he just call his market the Cho-Cho-Sing-Sang-Soo Market or whatever?

#3: Tradition. He's a traditionalist. And he loves America. Has a flag over every cash register. Picture of flag, too. Picture of *shop* with flag and picture of flag.

#1: That what I like about immigrants. They usually love America.

#5: Big Korean laugh.

#3: Well, be that as it may— *[Stares at #4]* Acceptable?

#4: Oh, yes. I'm always being that as it may. Just as I'm always leaping from one hand to the other. As the proverbial chipmunk might say—

#5: Kwong.

#3: Be that as it may, I broke the ten.

#1: My god.

#3: And got back eight something. *But*—and here's the rub—amongst that eight something was one of the very quarters I have here, now, on the table.

#2: Oh, hear, hear, flipsy-doodle, and wang the dong. That, undoubtedly, in some arcane manner, covers the first three-fifths of your life.

#3: Well, actually—if you can see it—it does. With more explanation, of course.

#1: I adore explanation. *My* mother was *always* explaining things to me. That's why I feel so secure in-in-in-in—

#5: Kwong!

#2: You've got the very *look* of security.

#1: And I feel it, too.

#2: Yes. Aunt Matilda's freckles. And her long summers at the shore.

#1: *Yes*. Her father *insisted* on five hours on the beach a day.

#3: He must have liked freckles.

#2: Used to call them freakles. *[She laughs]* What if we shifted everything just that much?

#1: She never forgot. She hated them, particularly since her father spoke so glowingly of his mother's milk-white skin. When she sat with me—

#4: His mother?

#1: No. Aunt Matilda.

#2: Oh, *that* explanation. Didn't you have *two* Aunt Matildas?

#1: Doesn't everyone?

#3: Yes. Say no more.

#1: Well, if you wish. I mean, not.

#4: I don't think I want to hear about the eight dollars and change either.

#2: Too long.

#4: Too complicated.

#2: Unless they link up.

#5: Freakles. Big Korean laugh.

#4: Careful with that link up business.

#1: A word?

#2: *Reverberations. —Link up*. Link up, my dears.

#1: *[Crying]* You never give me a chance.

#2: [Contritely] Will you help me with a gesture or two?

#1: No.

#4: A gesture's always good in circumstances, darling.

#3: I'll help.

#2: Profundimento!

#4: Don't you mean expressimo!

#1: She means shit!

#5: Big Korean laugh. Mroch!
    [They all laugh. In the following sequence, #2 directs the others into positions as she wishes]

#2: First, we do the singing bird. *[To #4]* Now you, Harry, up front and on all fours. *[To #1]* And you, Julie, straddle his neck and lie back. Push forward, make your crotch snug on his neck. Harry, put your hands on her feet.

#4: Are you sure this isn't some beast of burden?

#1: Or snuggle-cunt?

#2: *[Draping a cloth over them so that their heads show]* Now, lift up your head. *[She puts a beak on #4]* Squawk. *[He squawks]* Good. Julie, let your head hang so your hair flows.

#4: Am I a crow or a duck?

#1: Why is my head here?

#3: Always the essential question. May I bang a drum?

#2: Your head is a tail. Shake and wiggle it every now and then. Harry, you can be any bird you like.

#4: A sick crow, then.

#3: Let's hear it.
       [#4 caws like a sick crow. #1 laughs and shakes her head]

#1: Am I tickling you, Harry?
       [#4 caws]

#2: Now, Julie, hold your arms out.
       [She attaches wings]

#3: This is getting gorgeous.

#2: Okay. Julie, laugh.
       [#1 laughs]
Lightly.
       [#1 laughs lightly]
Harry, squawk.
       [#4 squawks]
Now, move. Flap your wings slowly.
       [They move, cawing, laughing, and flapping wings]

#3: Magnificent. The four-legged laughing sick crow with flowing tail and flapping wings. A gesture.

[They choreograph a few brief movements. #2 and #3 might accompany with music. #1 and #4 slowly collapse]

#4: This bird is dead.

#1: *[Flinging off covering, removing wings and rising]* Is that a poem? Do I hear a poem emerging?

#4: *[Rising but retaining his beak]* You do. Poem:

> This bird is dead.
> Caw!   Caw!
> When all is said
> And vision pales,
> This voice alone
> Speaks out once more
> Into this night—
> Caw!   Caw!
> This bird is dead.
> This bird is dead.

[He removes the beak and bows]
The song of the sick crow. No snuggle-cunt, let me tell you.

#5: Big Korean laugh. Piggy. Fungoo. Snuggle-cunt.
[The others clap]

#3: Magnifico.

#4: You bet.

#1: That was really very stimulating, Vera. Do you have more?

#2: What would you like?

#1: Well . . . how about my dying Aunt Edna?

#2: Good enough. Lyle?

#3: Am I Lyle?

#2: Yes. Front and center. Flossie?

#1: Am I Flossie?

#2: Yes.

#1: But you're still Jane?

#2: Yes. On his shoulders.
>   *[#1 gets on #3's shoulders. #2 removes her shoes and puts large white hands on her feet and hands. She then puts a large white old lady's head on #3 and large white hands over his hands]*
Now, fall back.
>   *[#1 dangles. Her feet-hands stick out in front of #3 and she dangles her own hands. #2 wraps a robe around their torsos so that on top we have #3's head and #1's feet-hands sticking out absurdly and #3's hands poking through. Below we have #1's head and hands. Since #3's legs and feet are dark, the effect is that of a two-headed torso with six hands]*
Good. Now, do it.

#4: Music?

#2: Not yet.
>   *[As #1 and #3 recite, they move appropriately so that one or the other is featured. The six hands, four of them mobile, are used to punctuate their lines]*

#1: I still feel very young.
>   *[#3 groans]*
I can smell the flowers.

[#3 groans]
I want love in my body.
[#3 groans]

#3: I was never young.
[#1 laughs]
I smell nothing.
[#1 laughs]
My body seeps life. Love is dead. I ache.
[#1 laughs]

#4: Music?

#5: Mroch! Dog Harry!

#2: No, no! Make a rock for them.
[He gets on his hands and knees]
Lean! Lean!
[#3 leans on #4 so that he and #1 form a diagonal line. #1's head rests on the stage]

#1: My ears are keenest to hear the bird's song.
[#3 groans]

#4: The crow?

#2: Yes. The crow.

#1: *[Repeating]* My ears are keenest to hear the bird's song.
[#3 groans. #4 caws like a sick crow. #1 laughs]

#3: This bird pecks through my veins. This bird leaves sores at every turn-ing.

#4: I can't be a rock, caw, and do the music all at once.

#2: Then *move!* I'll do the music.

[#4 slowly crawls, dragging #3 and #1 above and behind him]

#1: Oh, Aunt Edna. I always knew you loved the flowers.

#3: It was nothing!

#1: You had a life!

#3: I had no life. I got old and died. I was wormy.

#1: No. It was not like that.

#3: Nobody saw me.

#1: I saw you.

#3: How could you see me? We are one. I am in your bones.

#1: No. No. I am young.

#3: You are dying.

#1: No! No! See how I pluck at flowers?
       [She laughs. #3 moans]

#3: Too hard. It was too hard.
       [#4 caws like a sick crow]

#2: Good. Collapse slowly.
       [She takes out a flute and plays. #1 Continues to laugh, #3 to moan, #4 to caw until they collapse, the hands clutching]
Good. Let silence reign. Let silence reign.
       [Flute again. Lights down to one hand clutching. Pause. Lights]

#5: Big Korean laugh.

#4: The death and resurrection of Aunt Edna. Another gesture.

#1: The call of crows at early dawn.

#3: Dusk.

#5: Mroch!
     [They reassemble at the table]

#1: *[Crying softly]* I really loved her, you know. She really did hold me in her arms. That warmth has never left me.

#3: She had very hairy legs, I've heard.

#4: And why was she always called Phoebe?
     [Silence]

#3: That is a question never to be answered.

#5: Big Korean laugh.

#2: Would you like to do one more?

#4: It's rather wearing, you know. I am so many things.

#3: What else is there?
     [Pause]

#2: This one is restful. Everybody up.

#4: Aren't you managing a bit much?

#2: Well. I am the movement person. But you'll do in this pinch.

#5: Pinch! Pinch!

#2: You manage. *[To #3 and #1]* Do as I do, butts touching.
     [She takes off her shoes and lies on the stage, her legs up. They follow suit, legs in the center and up]

#4: Well, give me a clue, at least.

#2: Over there, the black cloth. Drape us.
    [#4 covers them so that legs and arms stick through]
The heads, now.
    [#4 puts a head with some torso and clothing on each foot, a mixture of male and female]
Improvise.

#4: Oh. Lights. Lights.
    [Lights down to the six heads, etc. Expression is limited to hands, leg flexions, and appropriate voices beneath the cloth. However, the hands may be misapplied. Heads H#3 and H#5 are male. During the exchanges #4 blows raucously on various horns, etc.]

H#1: So I said, Well, Doris, I realize you've been married for eight years and it's an absolutely rotten time to discover that—

H#2: Oh, don't, don't say it. Who ever believes in bisexual? Bivalvular, bi-vuncular, by jimminy—anything is more believable.

H#3: Oh. Bi-, bi-, bi-, ladies. Who, indeed, cares? Does he pay the rent? Does he miss the toilet bowl? Does he take out the garbage? Focus on what matters.

H#1: It's dandling my Jimmy, Jr. on his knee that I precisely don't want.

H#3: Then put a rug there, Persian, if you like. Dandle him in class as well as safety.

H#4: Oh, my dear, you really worry too much. My Richie has been dying for a promotion for years. And as you know, he's well, well qualified.

H#5: Your Richie, and mine, I'm sorry to say, is a poor little sucker at best.

H#4: Well, be that as it may, *someone* in a superior position wanted to dandle *him*, and he asked me what I thought he should do.

H#6: Well, good grief, what did you say?

H#4: Haven't said as yet. Thinking it over. Open for opinions.

#5: Hardly seems to matter, does it? Dandled or not, he's still the same poor bloody sucker, bloody pucker, pecker pucker, whatever.

H#4: Oh, how can you speak so of our Richie?

H#6: Oh, let Richie figure it out for himself.

H#4: Well, she's pressing him rather—

H#1 and 2: *She?*

H#6: End of that subject. Waste of our time. What are you doing about those awful odors in your back yards?

H#4: Actual muck in mine. Kids can't play there. Get sores. Disappear. Can't drink the water. Don't bathe. Slimy things.

H#3: And someone still wants to dandle your Jimmy?

ANYONE: And what is his real name? What is your real name?

H#4: Well, he is the oldest, you know.

H#1: I got a perm last week and two days later my hair started falling out. By the roots, by the roots.

H#2: The water, of course.

H#3: Put a rug on your head. Look better anyway.
        [They laugh]
Put a rug in the yard, too. Spray a bit. Pretty it up. Plug your nose. Stuff up your ass. Get with it.

H#4: We've solved the problem over our way. We go to the mall every day now.

H#3: That's the ticket. In the thick of the mall. They know about air there. Don't your Richie work there? Head gardener, snot-wiper or something?

H#4: Sales manager, please. In charge of wearables.

H#6: You mean condoms, douche-bags, and such?
    [They laugh]

H#4: No, Miss Belly-Fart. I mean dress wearables—for formal and semi-formal occasions.

H#5: Like mucking about the back yard. Cooking out, Weenies and beans. Here a sore, there a sore. . . .

H#3: Old MacDonald. Crafty old fart.
    [They laugh]

H#1: Oh, you men. So obscene.

H#3: As far as I'm concerned, MacDonald screwed every pig he had, and don't give me any oink, oink or moo, moo.

H#1: Do you think my hair is thinning? Do you really think it's the water? My scalp is scabby, too.

H#2: Of course it's thinning. You'll probably be bald and suppurating in a month. I hope you don't let them do your nails, too. They all have cancer there, you know.

H#1: But they're so beautiful, so well turned out and funny.

H#2: That's because they never leave. Haven't you noticed? IF they did, they'd die on the spot, pussy lumps all over them. They can't breathe normal air anymore.

H#5: The only normal air left is in damned Patagonia, and nobody lives there any longer. Few wild sheep, maybe. All carnivores now.

H#3: No mall.

H#5: No mail delivery. No tinkle of the ice cream truck.

H#1: Well, I don't like to complain.

H#4: What about the sump in your basement?

H#1: I don't do laundry there anymore.

H#4: Well, what is my Richie doing there so much?

H#5: Swimming lessons.
     [They laugh]
Him and the rats.
     [They laugh]
Tread water together. Kissy-kiss.

#5: Kissy-kiss.

H#2: Are you finishing your burgeroo, dear?

H#3: Can't. Damned teeth falling out. Last week gave up French fried. This week burgeroo. Next week, who knows?

H#5: Soup with a straw. Bean frappes.

H#2: You do have terrible gums. Kiss anybody?

#5: Kissy-kiss.

H#1: It's the water! *[Laughs hysterically]*

H#4: Well, what are we going to do about Richie?

H#5: Stuff him somewhere. Plug up a hole. Sump-strudel.

H#4: He's so ambitious.

H#2: Didn't he start out in *un*wearables?

H#4: No. Discardables and unmentionables. Condoms and suppositories. That's why he's so ripe for promotion. He's definitely very experienced.

H#3: That half-eaten burgeroo looks a little like him, don't you think?
    [They laugh]
That red oozing at the edges. Don't his gums leak?
    [They laugh]
Weren't there some Turks killed somewhere last week?
    [They laugh]

H#4: My whole house stinks.
    [They laugh]

H#6: I've worn the same underwear for six weeks.
    [They laugh]

H#3: And say, doesn't Richie have a sister?
    [They laugh]

H#1: The one who says she has a third leg?

H#5: Third tit, more likely. No ass, though.
    [They laugh]

ALL: *[Gradually subsiding]* Too much. Too much. Too much. Too much. . . . Jibber-jabber. . . .

H#1: Time for a nippy-nap.

H#2: A nappy nip.

H#3: Snoozeroo. Look for my teeth.

H#2: Sitting on them.
      [They laugh]

H#6: Amen.

H#2: A-man.

ANYONE: What's your name, honey?

#5: Snoozeroo.
     [They laugh softly and slowly collapse]

#4: *[Collecting the masks as the others come out from under]* Does this have a name?

#2: Yes. The Hydra of Babylon, Act I, Scene 1, The Neighborhood Gang.

#4: Engorging. And if you don't mind, I think I'll carry on a bit. We've had enough movement and gesture theory. I haven't had my proper input. I would like to say sweet nothings to someone in the interests of—

#5: Jibber-jabber.

#2: To whom, please?

#4: To someone named . . . Poo-Poo.

#1: Oh, may I be your Poo-Poo?

#4: Only if you're vulvular and red. Clam-hooked and dishy. And on my green grocer's weekly list.

#1: At the dropping of any hat. In a twixt. My gut is aching.

#5: Twixt. Dog Harry.
     [They speak the following like two lovers]

#4: Avast, then, your gut. Poo-Poo, I have long dwelled on your silvery lining.

#1: It slips and slides only for you, coagulant in crisis, cunning in sleep, and alluvial and pristine in my waking.

#4: Would that I could put my hand upon it, jellied membrane of my fevered dreams.

#1: Poo-Poo awaits your only touch, velvet inhibitor of my peristalsic rhythms.

#4: Movement divine. What nutrients course its winding path.

#1: Feel me. Feel me with thy slivery prickets. Feel, too, my granny's slippery slide into time. Tunnel my very bowels, repository of all my earthly love. Ingratiate yourself into me. Pluck and prod my petalled portals of desire, stroking your song as I become strong.

#4: And beast me any burden till your panting's done.

#1: Yes. Panting's from within, when all is kin and all the thrashing is blood-red. I gush, gush, gush for you.

#4: And feel you my hand?

#1: It moves as I move, and gives me something knuckled for my feed.

#4: Your hand can take my measure.

#1: And meld beyond all prissy constraint? —Yes, yes, kiss it I would if need arose.

#4: Then let it rise to your lips, my Poo-Poo.

#1: Oh, flow, flow. I am river to your questing.

#4: Hard, hard on. Valve and valve. I have a question, spurting prisms all for you.

#1: And that is?— Speak it. Speak.

#4: May I— May I—

#1: Quick! Your Poo-Poo comes all creamy and new to the world.

#4: May I take you . . . *to the movies?*

#1: *[With a sigh of relief and release]* Ahhhhhh! In the mall, if you would. Only in the mall.

#3: *[Rising]* Poo-Poo and Popo Go to the Movies. A scene.
    [Music by #2 and #3 as #1 and #4 hold their pose a few moments]

#5: Popo. Popo. Kissy-kiss. Jibber-jabber.

#4: *[Returning to the table]* I wish I had known earlier I was Popo. It would have made all the difference.

#2: As anything would.

#4: You mean—?

#2: Do you think a Mary ever lives like a Margaret?

#4: No more a mouse than a midget.

#3: A mousse than a mole.

ANYBODY: If only we knew their real names.

#3: —Back to the eighty-seven cents and the newspaper I bought. What did I read?

#2: That the Orinoco was dry.

#3: Yes. And the savages along its banks were sad. The crocodiles died off. And children ate beetles.

#4: But it wasn't first page news.

#3: No. It never is. But it set my blood boiling. It made . . . an unmeasurable difference.

#4: For you.

#3: Yes.

#1: What about the other forty-nine articles or so? Did they do nothing?

#3: I read half of them. Half. But it would take a week to finish what Orinoco did to me. Indirectly, of course. Indirectly. Directly, there were other things, millions of other things.

#4: And only to you.

#1: Like my grandmother. Unless you dug her grave and sucked on her bones you'd never know me. I barely know myself. Her grandmother's grandmother had the oddest nose.

#2: Do you know her name?

#5: Mroch!

#3: I still dream of those mud-caked banks, with eerie amphibian heads sticking out. There were tunnels there, and a fast-holding life in the depth and the dark. But the savages sit blindly in the sun, their skin flaking away from their bones. They make an occasional sound.

#1: Like?
      *[#2 and #4 make the faces and sounds of savages on the muddy
      bank of a dried river in the sun]*
It's not like a frog or a snake or sick dog.

#3: No. It's more the sound of rotten tree cracking, dry skin splitting, popping pus, wind in winding tunnel, jungle mumble.

#1: Like breath going out?

#3: And out. Never back. Never back. Some were dead sitting there. But not their eyes. Glazed and nearly unblinking they were food for blowy flies. But they knew something. The eyes knew the river was down, dried and gone. They heard the fish flapping and heard the large birds squawk as they swooped.
     [#2 and #4 squawk]

#1: I can see them. How they fight and tear over the food.

#3: And other creatures slide and crawl down to the sucky mud and clamp on bird.
     [More sounds from #4 as #2 rises and imitates sound and movement]
Leg pulled out. Snapped. Eye plucked. Bloody, bloody feathers. This they watched, skin-bag babies on their knees. Flaps of breast with black dry nipple. Orinoco raisins.

#1: These birds—are they—?

#3: Another ceremony? Yes.

#1: For what?

#4: What page was this article on?

#3: I estimate that these thoughts, these images, used upwards of 289 million brain cells a second, bubbling and mixing in millions of ever-expanding unpredictable combinations over forty-nine seconds or so. In other words, if you built me the finest computer, thirty stories high and six blocks long, you might, assuming no accident or miscalculation, you might, after a year or so of work, reproduce two or three percent of the possible system that caused what appear to be those thoughts for those seconds, allowing of course for myriad nuances and reflections I haven't experienced or even consciously noticed, all this the consequence of insignificant me reading one article, if you could really call it an article, not even on page one during a single inconsequential blip in my inconsequential life in this consequential void.

#4: And would you trade a fraction of your brain for that shining simulacrum, that preposterous and glittery reduction?

#3: I wouldn't trade my spit for it.

#4: Why?

#3: Because I wouldn't itch anymore. My spit lives. And I love to itch.

#1: What I want to know is why did the Orinoco dry up? Where are the mud puppies of yesteryear? And what, now, is our ceremony?

#2: *[Rising]* Poem: Where Are the Mud Puppies of Yesteryear?
    [As she recites, the others accompany her with bubbling noises and flute sounds]

> Where are the mud puppies of yesteryear,
> Gill-less now in their graves?
> No more does Orinoco flow;
> No more do mighty waves
> Lave those flats where puppies played
> And night was cricket's music.
> The savages on banks arrayed,
> Bright teeth in shriveled gum,
> Pursue blind gods and destinies;
> And long-billed birds,
> Their stalking stilled,
> Life killed and panorama stayed, stayed,
> Are monuments in suckless mud,
> Dry feathered sticks,
> To greed and enduring silence.
> Where are the mud puppies of yesteryear?

    [She dances appropriately as the sounds and music continue, a dance of loss and death. A few moments of silence]

#5: Big Korean laugh. Burgeroo. Mroch! Mroch!

#4: May we know about the worthless item you bought to gratify your vanity?

#3: Ah. You mean, of course, the fourth transaction?

#4: Indeed, I do.

#1: I have a sneaking suspicion there were more than four transactions that lead to the eighty-seven cents in your pocket.
[They laugh]

#1: Do you keep your hand in your pocket much?
[They laugh]

#3: You're a card, my dear.

#4: The vanity, please.

#2: Worm-juice for his armpits.

#3: Yes. To insinuate me where I wish.

#1: My Aunt Edna once said quite seriously that I was vain.

#3: And Aunt Edna's in you.

#1: *[Searching]* Yes. These three or four inches are Edna that day.

#2: And you were–?

#1: Five, maybe seven or ten.

#4: And she said—?

#2: *[Becoming Aunt Edna]* Oh, child, my child, you'll become wicked if you don't think more.

#1: *[A young girl, crying]* Oh, don't say that. What do you mean? I'm *not* wicked.

#2: No. Not yet. Do you know what you did to Harold?

#1: I gave him a lemonade and a cookie.

#2: You didn't hear a word he said.

#1: He spoke?

#2: He told you something very secret, something . . . dreadful that happened to him.

#1: And what did I do?

#2: You left him in the middle of a sentence.

#1: Why?

#2: To get a new toy. You wanted to show him.

#1: Did he like it?

#2: He never saw it. You became distracted. You never came back.

#1: And he—?

#2: He cried. First because he told you and second because you didn't listen, you didn't hear. Third, because you didn't come back.

#1: Why didn't he *make* me listen?

#2: Harold wasn't like that.

ANYONE: I wonder what his real name was.

#1: And what happened?

#2: Nothing. He simply isn't your friend as much as he was. Forever.

#1: Then *he's* wicked.
    [#3 sticks out his tongue at her and makes a sound]
Are you Harold?

#3: I've changed my name many times. But yes, once I was Harold.

#1: [Herself again] Well, you could have fooled me.

#3: I fool everybody. Everybody fools everybody. And everything.

#1: Was there more to Orinoco?

#3: Oh, much, much more. But I read other articles, you know.

#4: And there's still *your* vanity.

#1: I'm not interested in the other articles. Not now, anyway. Tell me more about Orinoco.

#3: Mighty Orinoco?

#1: Whatever. I feel it is where we are going. It is where the birds at last alight. The last horizontal.

#3: *[Declaiming]* Who can say what Orinoco knows?

#2: I can.

#3: You?

ANYONE: And won't you tell us your real name?

#2: The *birds* I know. Not the savages passing foul wind upon foul wind upon the bank. Not their oozing skin. Not their dismembered thought. Nor the babies with fly-filled holes for eyes and worms crawling in their nostrils, tunneling into brain. No, none of that. But of the birds, yes. Beaky, stilty

creatures of dark unmeaning eyes. Rustling feathers shaking loose a thousand fleas, no pattern alike. When the water went and the fish lay exposed, vibrating into death, the mud not really welcoming, they moved and they swooped silently down and gobbled, gobbled, until between the mud and their fat bellies, they could not lift. *What is a bird that cannot lift?* Think of it Picture it. *What is a bird that cannot lift?* And other creatures, furred and scaly-skinned, slid down and clamped on bloaty gizzard, squished the juices out, sucked and swallowed tangled pieces, leaving clotted feather, broken beaks for other orders. A few disgorged their feed and lifted off the flat, flew hungrily and sick away, mad-squawking, mad-squawking—
    [The others squawk]
into brush, to come another day to other succulence. Those creatures I know. —And on the shore, dry rattling that passed for laughter—
    [Dry rattling: a tableau behind the table: masks]
as heads exploded from the mirth, and globes of worms shriveled quickly in the sun. These I do not know, but only observe.
    [Silence]

#5: Poo-Poo.

#1: *[Removing her mask]* Is this the kind of thing that Harold spoke and I heard not?

#2: *[As Aunt Edna]* You were foul, foul! Even then.

#1: But I was a child. I am still a child.

#2: You were old enough to know what pain was. And you neither heard nor saw the pain. That was your vanity, creeping under your skin.

#3: And my vanity, what was that, my fourth and last transaction?

#2: *[Herself again]* That vanity we shall tell.
    [She points dramatically to #4]

#4: As you wish.
    [As #4 speaks, #2 and #1 perform as follows: they tie opposite

right legs together and encase their torsos with a shawl, robe, or blan-
ket. Their arms are not visible or free. They wear a rooster's and a hen's
head. The effect is of one body with two heads, dancing. The lines and
the dancing alternate. The two heads articulate sound and action. The
music is tango and may be recorded.]

The Secret Hen Vanity: a title, a drama, a story, a conflict, a puzzle, and—
Once there was a crooked cock.
   [Cock calls]
That loved a crooked hen.
   [Hen clucks]
The cock the hen his cockscomb pled.
   [Cock pleads]
the hen the cockscomb quickly bled.
   [Hen attacks]
Cockroo, cockroo, the cock cried out.
   [Cock shrieks]
Cuckoo, cuckoo, the hen cried back.
   [Hen deceitful]
But soon the cock no longer crew
The hen that once he thought he knew
Was gone before his bloodied eyes.
   [Cock disillusioned, cock blind and bleeding, cock dying]
Behold, before us, cock, he dies.
   [Cock's head collapses]
Cuckoo, cuckoo, the hen she lies.
   [Hen clucks]
Cuckoo, cuckoo, the hen she lies.
   [Hen clucks]
      [They are still. Music. Silence.]

#3: *[Angrily]* Unfold that vanity! *I am too naked!*
      [#4 unfolds #2 and #1. Fowl heads off]

#1: *[Sympathetically]* But it was only *then.*

#3: *Then? Then?* Do you think *then* is ever *gone?*

#1: But if never gone, what is then?

#3: *Now.* Now and forever. The world always *is.* Every moment dies and becomes.

#1: *[Enlightened]* Like my Aunt Edna?

#2: Like your *dead* Aunt Edna.

ALL: *[Singing]* Hallelujah! Hallelujah!

ANYONE: Did anyone ever know her real name?

#1: I can say that I know the birds now, but of course I've always known them. The birds are but one face of what we've all always known. These three pores my dear Aunt Edna? How frail I speak. This tooth is she. So many forever drops of my blood. My skin I shed. Daily it rubs off me. But Aunt Edna stays. Who else? What remote intransigencies crack my bones? And who would be a fool to name them? I have pleistocene affinities, and I can dance a savage between my moments. Oh, what a work am I, what a bubbling mystery, what frothy incorporations. *[To #3]* And could you really love me, knowing all that, *guessing* all that? What monster would *dare* to know me?

#3: I could make you a part of my miscellany, if you wish, some cosmic clash amid the teacups.

#1: And would you call it love?

#3: As much as any remnant bespeaks me, casts a shadow on my life. Only I would with force of will, for this or that moment, impose upon it a certain sacrament, invest it with a charm to further provoke my passion. What else is love? What else is anything?

#4: Precisely. Listen to you. With words do you create this sentience. Oh, granted you have smelled her and some quirky chemistry seems your motivation, but could you love without the words?
    [#1 rises]

#2: Could they love without minutest prickles of the skin, observed by only their eyes? Look how her lower lip speaks to him. See the subtle grace of her hip for him.
       [#3 rises]

#4: And does he nothing?

#2: He gives promise of filling her voids.

#4: And he has none?

#2: There are voids and voids.

#4: Show me.
       [As #2 speaks, she positions #1 and #3 in a number of positions, none of them conventionally erotic]

#2: Void #1. Humps in the world. Have you ever seen a hump and not recognized it? All humps break the surface, mar the plane. All humps rise. The world cannot disguise humps. Humps give themselves away.
       [#3 is bending forward, with his hands on the stage, his hips high. #1, nearby, is doing a back bend, her pelvis arched high. #2, with her last line, flings up #1's skirt]
Void #2. Limb-shaking. As apple trees their apples shed, so too these lovers when they bed. Do you see the twitch of her leg? His more forceful. And how they look. Her arm, oiled by a shoulder under-haired, moves in just a way that his brain is all musky tendrils. Now watch his fingers. Is he dying? No. But in clutching the air, stabbing into space he—

#4: But what is all this giving off? What apples are falling?

#2: Whatever fills this void. No apple rots. Even heads are limbs.

#4: Heads?

#5: Jibber-jabber!

#2: They lose their natural motion. The mouth has no control. The eyes are cocked and droop and cross. Look, have you ever seen such an assemblage?
    [#1 and #3 are twitching, shaking, quivering, etc.]

#4: A void indeed. No museum could contain it. Let the apples roll.

#2: Would you like to try for #3.

#4: I? You would trust me?

#1: Why not, if you let me speak?
    [#4 rises]

#4: Dare I do the birds? Can they be a void? We come back always to the birds. Did they fly when man was but a hint, a new beating thunder and shadows on the earth?

#1: Combine it with the mouth.

#4: Yes. There, truly, is a void. It spits out speech and consumes—

#2: Do it!
    [Lights down to just the mouths of #1 and #3]

#4: Suck!
    [#1 does a repertoire of sucking]
Suck is what takes in. Suck is noise. Suck is wet. Suck is dangerous. Suck is lips. Suck is measureless movement. Suck is what is sucked. Suck is promise of interior. Suck is unction. Suck is mystery. Suck is ecstasy. Suck is womb. Suck is mud. Suck is suck. Suck, suck, suck. Let us pause.
    [Pause]
Tongue!
    [#3 does a repertoire of tongue movements]
The tongue can quickly dart, like bird peeping from nest. Or tongue can grossly fill the mouth, be softly choking flesh, palpating moistly for a fly to land. It can waggle forthrightly, to furthest extent, saucy and naughty as a

new shoot. And it can lewdly lick, give evidence of lubrication for all our fitful starts. Game licks are often prelude to fancied results. As sound will tell you.
>   *[Lights up]*

#2: Well done.

#4: It was enough?

#2: Enough as ever. We'll end her with an exit processional, the double-humped dromedary. You do the music.
>   *[#2 arranges #1 and #3 thus: both on hands and knees, #3 with head under #1's dress and between her legs. Both humped. Covered or not. Music. They crawl backstage slowly, #4 whinnying, snorting, etc. as they crawl]*

Void, void, and more void. Void, void, and more void. Double void and triple. Void. Void. Void.
>   *[Silence as the lights dim. Then up, as they reassemble]*

#3: I think I can say at this point that I am refreshed. But not enough to explore further any fourth transaction.

#4: What about the token you needed to travel?

#3: Somehow I knew you'd ask about that.

#1: No birds in the subway.

#2: *Are there not?*
>   *[Pause, as they are visualizing them]*

#5: Big Korean laugh. Twixt. Poo-Poo. Suck.

#1: And what kind of man would buy four cucumbers and a turnip?

#2: One who would make a soup.

#3: When I was young I counted lights between the stations. As if my life depended on it. Now I count the mice *in* the station. Waiting for trains is never dull. The mice dart in and out. The tracks are littered. Their bellies are fat, but they hasten no less. Do you know that mice can climb a vertical surface? Does anyone know, or care, how many teeth in a mouse's mouth?

#2: I'm thinking that another day you might have no change or only bills or eighty-six or ninety-one cents, representing who knows what eons of your infinite life, what labyrinths of connection.

#3: True. And only one pocket at that. How old were my socks, did my nostrils run and why, what twitch in my liver, and what were the people around me wearing? Doing? Thinking? It was all mine. How can I bear it all unless I embrace and proclaim a certain studied stupidness, dullness, life-lessness?

#2: Tell us about the beggars.

#3: That day?

#2: Yes. The day of the eighty-seven cents in your pocket. Skip the mice, even though I've questions.

#3: I'll skip a thousand things.

#2: I know.

#3: Very well. But you'll have to help me.

ANYONE: Won't you tell us your name?

#1: Do you ever stop to think that some of those mice are *related*? That some are young mice and some old mice? That there are males and females? Why don't I ever see a normally dead mouse? Why don't I ever see a normally dead bird? There are all these living things around me and unless they're stuck on fly-paper, crushed or hit by a car, caught in a trap, poisoned or something like that, I never see them dead.

#5: Mroch! Mroch! Kissy-kiss!

#4: Well, I think you might find a vocation there, if you thought about it, a purpose in your life. After all, what does "stuck on fly paper" really mean? Who isn't a fly?

#1: I know they eat each other and rot away. But not all at once. Where are the rotting and half-eaten bodies? And do they eat each other, eat their own kind? Do mice eat dead-from-old-age or diseased mice? Are mice mice-eaters? Do they ever die from old age? What are the childhood diseases of mice? Why don't we ever *cry* for mice?

#4: You're asking some very key questions, Genivieve. Some others are why is a question a question, when is a story, and who killed cock-mouse at the crossroads?

#5: Kwong! Fungoo!

#1: Of course some animals are vegetarians. But still, they could lick the blood or whatever oozes out. What's the point of burying anyone? —Would you eat me?

#4: You mean—?

#1: If you were hungry, of course. And if I were dead.

#4: Perhaps. If you were healthfully dead.

#3: You mean a clean, healthy-looking corpse.

#4: Yes. Not like the subway.

#3: Those mice are vermin-filled.

#4: And on the trains?

#3: Ah, yes. The beggars.

[They take turns at being beggars, always laughing at whoever is begging]

#1: I would never eat a dirty rat.

#2: You're already eating dirty rats. And dirty rats are licking your rotting body.

#3: *[Pulling up his pants, revealing ulcers on his leg. Pathetically]* I'm dying! I can't pay for my medicine! I'm hormone-deficient! My shit is green!

#1: Paint with it.

#4: Pick scabs.

#3: It's no joke!

#4: It is a joke. *[To #1]* Would you lick his leg?

#2: *[Revealing a large, wrinkled breast from the middle of her chest]* I live in a shelter! There's no milk! *[Looking at #5]* My baby is sick all the time! Crying all the time! *[She cries like a baby]*

#3: How old is he?

#2: Don't know!

#3: How long have you been trying to feed him?

#2: Don't know!

#1: I'll bet she gets picked up in a baby carriage every day.

#2: *[Pulling up a sleeve and showing arm]* I'm clean! I'm clean!

#3: Shove it. Shove it.

#2: He's twenty-seven! *[Pushing her breast forwards]* Here. Try it.

#5: Fat-toe.

#4: Better than a dead mouse, Nancy.

#2: Try it! Try it!
   [She rips off the breast and beats them with it]
Try it!

#1: *[One foot bent under, limping]* Raped by her own father! Foster homes! Child abuse! Asthma! Hole in heart! Pee through my nose! Divorced!

#3: Give her a mouse.

#4: Two.

#2: *[Seriously]* Give her what she needs.

#4: And what is that?

#2: *[To #1]* What is it you need?
   [#1 struggles to speak, cannot. She gags, drools, moans incoherently, pees through her mouth]

#4: Well, so much for that.

ANYONE: Does she have a real name?
   [#1 sits]

#4: Well, Harold. So that was your day of the eighty-seven cents in your pocket. And what did it do for you?

#3: I wish to god I knew. But people are always telling me. Change your underwear daily. Think straight. Love nature. Changes every day.

#1: And where does that leave us?

#4: Precisely—

#2: *Here.*

#3: Here?

#2: Here.

#3: And where is here?

#2: Here is where first we dance—
        [#1 and #3 dance a quick dance of cripples]
And then we die.
        [#1 and #3 scream]

#4: Surely you can put it better. A song about blind pigeons, maybe. Nipple-stealing insects in the night? I dreamed a worm crawled in my left nostril or the agate in my liver/the liver in the river?

#2: Here is a theater, a mirror, a world.

#4: A mirror without glass.

#2: Here is the time now and everything up to now.

#4: What a noble load is that.

#2: Here is a game, a rite, an occasion, an indulgence, a delusion, a madness, an exhibition, a hope, an escape, a conspiracy, a diversion, a diversity, a conundrum, a pain, a boredom, a deceit—

#5: *[With accumulated ferocity and lunacy, in any order or repetition, from the words he has been accumulating. The others may or may not echo, at any volume, some or all of his words, the only time they take note of him/her. They may also blast away on their instruments]*

Cucamunga!
Dipsy-doodle!

Fungoo!
Kissy-kiss!
Higgledy-piggledy!
Dog-dog!
Big Korean laugh!
Mroch!
Warty!
Dipsy!
Dog Harry!
Cucamunga!
Fungoo!
Piggy!
Kwong!
Fungoo!
Snoozeroo!
Fat-toe!
Suck!
Burgeroo!
Moustache!
Moustache!
Kwong!
Jibber-jabber!
Cucamunga!
Yellow pus!
Popo!
Freakles!
Piggy!
Doodle-doodle!
Mroch!
Yellow pus!
Fungoo!
Poo-Poo! Poo-Poo!
Big Korean laugh!
Dog-Dog! . . .

#1 and #3: *[Screaming]* STOP!
         [Silence]

#2: Of course. Everyone has to say stop now and then. To build society and civilization. For respite. But it always creeps back in.

#3: What creeps back in?

#5: *[Subdued]* Cacamunga.

#2: What the blind blackies saw on the river bank.

#1: Blackies?

#5: *[Subdued]* Cacamunga.

#2: Were they white?

#1: They saw nothing.

#2: Can you believe that?

#1: Of course I can.

#2: Good. Then you can understand their patience in the face of it all.

#1: *[Humorously]* Me no understand nothing.

#3: Me just poor pecky bird.
    [He begins to imitate in sound and movement the long-legged, long-billed birds on the dried river flats. #1 joins in, both gradually acquiring beaks, wings, etc. Music. #4, then #2 put on the native masks, make dry gutteral sounds, behind which sounds #2 and #4 in a litany, as the lights slowly dim]

#2: Poor pecky bird.

#4: Peck, peck.

#2: Poor pecky bird.

#4: Peck, peck.

#2: River bed dry.

#4: Water go.

#2: Mud no sucky.

#4: Peck, peck, bird.

#2: Sun come hot.

#4: Burn, pecky bird.

#2: Fish all dry.

#4: Choke, pecky bird.

#2: Poor pecky bird.

#4: Peck, peck, bird.

#2: Pecky bird scratch.

#4: Bleed, pecky bird.

#2: Pecky bird still.

#4: Die, pecky bird.

#2: Poor pecky bird.

#4: Peck, peck.

#2: Poor pecky bird.

#4: Peck, peck.

#2: Peck, peck.

#4: Peck, peck.

#2: Peck, peck.

#4: Peck, peck.

> *[Repeat. A backdrop slowly descends: a quaint cottage with garden, flower boxes in window, dog in doorway, pastoral scene beyond, etc. The birds, #1 and #3, gradually become still. Finally, just the gutteral noises accompanied by the music. Completely dark. Just visible in the background, flashes of "comedy" and "laugh" just barely lighting up the masks]*

CURTAIN

THE
QUI PARLE
POEMS

Note:
The *Qui Parle Poems* are based on lines from
the preceding *Qui Parle* play.

Prefatory

these are the *qui parle*
who wither in all light
all speech is for the dark
where utterance finds its mark
so erringly

our cunning is but our proof
of solidarity with the lost
non speech is for the wicked
rippling with scars
pariahs of light

we affirm
only as we sink
words
are the lost cause we thrive on

To Say It I

were to say it
nothing

three screech and a turnip
who is that

the crease in my pants
has a long history
twenty years gone
who could care

I have a mindless hum
never repeated
collocating
wisps of flesh
quaint memory
hope and
the weight of years

have you heard it

give me a business letter
call me mr. x
measure my shoes

closer is further
but better comfort
life is to be recognized
not lived

Pond-Pundle

game licks are often prelude to fancied result
lubricious lucubrations
that break tangled night
and glide smoothly into dawn

tongue can lick lips
and swank like a proud duck
with shaky tail

squawk like a morning bugle
rousing sluggish limbs
to day's full plunge

duck-wet
is a musk
we swing on

and ring the turtle
to no time
no time

Bird Call

my ears are keenest to hear the bird's song
far or near
in cadence strange or tuneless call
buffeting a timeless space
between it and me

in that space
figures of a life can dance
their true form
for no one to see

pale other life
sometimes dreams
sometimes stutters to a halt
half-dazed with a sliver sight
shudders forgets sleeps again

and wakes
to squawky melodies
tooty tread
and vast suspicion
of bed

Pecky Bird

this bird pecks through my veins
leaves sores at every turning
I dare not hear its squawk

through jagged beak
my blood would seep
and make a rain
upon my life

best bet to plug my ears
pretend to silence
coax the pain

and if it should stop
should pecky bird transgress
perhaps my luck
to sink soundlessly
never hearing its mad mad aria
so bloody and joyful to be free

Tea

panting's from within
and strips a chord clean

like fear's sweat
and dying's moan

exhaled
they mingle
dilute in baser realm

and when reported
provoke snicker or yawn
sometimes serious conversation
on a lawn

The Last Vanity

when shall we tell our last vanity
our gums revealed and eyes
no longer focused on the real

the real that shimmers in a light
that is not light is all
that we have loved

loved but never held that real
we are reluctant to unclasp
and launch upon another sea

I see expanse but never form
nor bird far-flying
no regal token no breath

listen closely for mine
the last will say
false in a falsity
one breath more
one breath more

Crows At Early Dawn

the call of crows at early dawn
is a summons never heeded

for should we tread through wetted grass
and into woods where they have flown

our journey's end might be a clearing
filled with absence

and as we dried marking sun's slow rise
the measure of our distance would be lost

we should stand alien and alone
until honk or scream brought beating
back to our stilled heart
and pathways opened

our lives are crows never followed
never found

beaky stilty creatures

they sit on mud
their webby feet welding
to the drying element

the flow is gone
few creatures slither
their eyes see but care not

green canopy dries
the sky scorches
feathers ooze last drops

were someone there to hear
there would be hoarse weak croaks
before night fell

in the dark
even whisper of a breeze
makes feathers hum

they cannot fall
their eyes will never close
time is dead

Another Day To Other Succulence

let us leave these dry shores
bereft of even scaly life
barren of green

inward
there is an interior
where sun never sets

there
blinking in confusion
we may slake and we may feed

trust the distant shriek abate
the buzz decline
new lushness grow from death

and we may crawl
make the trek
and squat and squawk anew

Requiem

for all our fitful starts
there are mangled conclusions
within which we dimly shape
the face of things

hard mirror of a life
we catch the breath
in time to bury

stare love
as it stiffens

and crackle out a laugh
in the waning light

All Humps Rise

the world cannot disguise humps
humps give themselves away
humps break the surface mar the plane

true sight sees never level
lacks formality
can lie only in the blink

hence sleep and death

for other we are red-rimmed
achy with fixation
tight-wired to brain

vision is the gift of the cursed

Poo-Poo And Popo
Go To The Movies

and make a jell of it

she sticks to his hair
and he burbles incoherently
with big teeth

Poo-Poo has one big breast
but the small one has the nipple

Popo makes rat-calls
plucks the ukulele
and pees in his pants
while Poo-Poo screams and screams

they are sitting in the lap of an audience
collectively squeezed
until their tongues stick out purple

during a lull they drool
lap up the melting chocolate
and whisper sweet nothings

the movie has a lagoon in it
the star is unrobed
the audience blows up

Pleistocene Affinities

sometimes
when I dance a savage between my moments
I implode
with frothy incorporations

my utterings
are full of backwash
estuarial creepings
and night croak

was I an eye
that ever looked at green density
with longing

did I look back at muck
and wonder

was my brain a seedling

there are moments of stillness and of silence
when I am lidless and intense
when heart beats oddly
and fingers scratch slowly
more powerful than thought

yes I could rip a throat
plunge a bloody belly
heave with ocean force

my citadel has many windows
my vistas are vaster
than any clock can tick
my breath reeks of stagnant flats

o brother scorpion brother rat
do you also
hear my song

The Speaker

who is it that speaks
is it the little brown bear
furry behind my tongue
is it the tiddlywink
immobile and substantial on the floor
can it be my great-aunt's morning ache
of no discernible cause
devouring me since my birth

I cannot say who or what speaks
only that my ears have tendrils
slivery filaments
that poke my earthly space
like so many nomads

is it you they ask of the wall
peeling a century of paint
can it be you
they say of the odd light through the window

they tangle me everywhere
make monstrous my ears
pull me dank and dark
bring back a thousand screams

but rooted they are in me
some raw core of my being
and all their vibrations
bespeak unholy me
dangling
breathless
exquisitely poised

to hear to know if I can
who what in what way
is it that speaks
who is it that speaks

Pain

what is the word pain when you hear it
do you see the prison it is locked in
will you go there
knowing no key can let you out

pain is a pair of eyes
staring out at dark that has no day
pain has no measure but the feeler
who is mute

speak pain lose pain
speak pain and a hand will hold you
soothing and ignorant

silence is the only way to keep pain whole

Ceremony For A Bird With A Large Head And A Small Body

when it flies
the head droops
seeking earth

should it alight
its body feels crushed
by the weight upon it

all navigation is doomed
no flight lifts or soars
only cumbersome passage
from here to there

a final rest
unpredictable
no cairn no mound
faceless heap
to no music

just silence and space

Commentary

every book every written
has another between the lines

we read and are read
and end even
the living and the dead

two lovers
on a burial bed

To Speak Or Not

we may say everything stops
or nothing stops
stop is a word
as love is a word
or pain or death
everything is a word
and we may change our words

what then really happens
when we drop the words
what is there

if we sink beneath our articulations
which tell us nothing
what sound do we make
how does our body move
which crepitations formulate love
do we expire with a hiss

between my words and being
lies an empire
of few conquistadors and no army

when we visit transgress
the only question is is it
the only respite
what is not

nothing is the pale everything
we dream on

bright other
only terror

Warty Night

give me the finger
with the hair

croak me your song
lift your hind leg

this night empties fast
of passion

but residue of scent
some febrile tremor
concocts a point
to which I bend

in the squish of dead end
I gulp breath
after breath of any air
call you my fair
pluck out a sigh
like an eye

and dream on

So Be You And I

frog-eyed and pouty-lipped
you were queen of the pond

and I
sleek as a snake
smiled over-broadly
found you
wet spirit of the water
incorporate musk
dank message of love
as trill found nodding chorus

so let heron pluck
let water drain
and desiccation reign

some moments are history and love

Twisty Fingers Like Grim Fate

your life was ten thousand nights
of back flow
numb hands
fumbling overhead
on rugs of no message
mindless repetition

when you brought your gnarled hands into bed
did they tingle
from blood's slow return
did they weave forgotten lore
cast off the carapace
and gently palpate another song
another time another place

or could they not
crusted and constrained
by blood's long servitude
and time's attrition

did they touch like tusk
only roughen with love
and tremble spasm after spasm
to no delight
no issue

Death Small And Large

there is no imperative
that death grow monstrously
sometimes there is only a squeak
or a stiffening of the fingers

death grown large
is often regal
pain a trumpeting
of departure

no ceremonies
glaze small deaths

she walked through a door
and wasn't there
he swallowed one last piece of bread
and simply stared
something burst softly while they slept

no stage
but nullity
blank schedule
something quickly written in

Edge

beware the jagged edges
in the contour of your days

blind repetition
dulls the rim
as dullness blurs

history is the keeping
of such follies
we make ourselves conform

o ragged outline
o bloody points
could I both live
and also bear your ecstasies

Dog Harry Speaks

I have felt Dog Harry's hot breath
reeking upon me

his teeth are yellow
and he laves me with his salivation

eyes bloody
and a nose encurdled
he stares
not at but through me
at something other

I am the thing he passes through
my dumb vibration
the refracton of his voice

Tally

nought fraught
the light
the laughing
or the lividity

all accounts
in reckoning

when the book is in
the only cover is in it
all to all
one life one death

This Night Inviolate

let this one night be inviolate
neither prison of my flesh
nor posture of my soul

instead let utterance
inarticulate
and let time dissolve
beyond all boundary

mere love will fecundate
allotted time
for now this one night
shred my skin
burst my brain
exalt me
with pregnant nothing

Message

I am lighter than feathers
when you salivate

public or private
early or late
your moistening
quickens flight

hang-dog though you look
and wall-eyed
those dripping beads of lust
trigger my lack
project a feathery plush
and gather all seeming
in a rush
to beat back night

Gesture

all gestures live in a different space
where we are strangers
mutated otherness
pale reprise

holding an elbow
we proffer a kiss
mindless of the dancing rest

we pick our way
have a meager say
while gesture rides away

to a land of vast residue

Thinker

a body in deliberation
bears no watching

the thought expressed
has jelled the form

idea
projects a norm

at loss
are both

one faded image
fades another

collocates defeat

From Here To There

translation is always dangerous
unless loosely spoke
the five rung ladder
functions four
in travel
and sits oddly on the ear

that quirk approximation
hints an affirmation
meaning with loss

the universal application

If It's Not One Thing It's Another

when is a frog a turtle
or a bee a beast

yes I love you
but the sky is blue

beggars to do-nuts
you can read me
any way you want

precisely
it's not one thing
it's another

always
is where you'll find me

never

Market

there's a big Korean laugh
at my fruit market

between its teeth
I pick the pears

he says he's Kwong
to me he's Cho-Cho-Sing-Song-Soo
because I like his walk

you sell me peach?
he picks his teeth

his pants like mine are baggy
but eyeballs lock across a frosty space

four peach dollar
I offer two

you peach-head fella
yes I peach-head fella
and you big fella Kwong

he smiles
you suck on peach you hear

I hear all right
I hear a big Korean laugh

A Gesture In Time

a gesture's always good
in circumstances

impresses time
collates the blurring focus

so we may see and love
the creature we have made

and gnawing on our leg or not
we easily see that we have got
the better
of the less of things

and stroke the beast

Why I Can't Be A Rock, Caw, and Do The Music All At Once

because I am at the heart of a stillness
that is fear
no mirror reflects
and voice unspeaks me

I would be a rock
if I could wheel my body in a barrow
never stopping

or a crow
if I could feel my pulsing throat
and savage the world

doing the music requires six hands
I sing from the wrong end
and a tootle's as good as a toot

tell me to quiver indivisibly
blink once in a hundred years
and moan like no wind

and I'm your man
or whatever

Henrietta

clam-hooked and dishy
she was poised for a fling

from the dock it was dicey
till she dug in for nicey

coagulant in crisis
but jellied membrane
of all my fishy dreams

raw turtle
dove of love
shoal-scrapings

heave from reel
how she flies
how it lies
how it dies dies

great squish in the morning

Night Weight

beast me any burden
till your panting's done
I'll rise to any bait
and ever wait
consumption's proof in boggle time

there clock will pause
and slowest hare
will ring the tortoise
we two will mortise
walls to hold this night
this fevered night
and make our stand

Disclosure, I

give me something knuckled
for my feed
raw teeth can shred
better than a baby's suck
or lover's bead

when life is but death's waiting
every moment stabs
for knowing that will savage

lying on your milky breast
I bleed
surcease
is but the lull before I storm

hold me and forgive
I am mortal's pawn

Disclosure, II

your hand can take my measure
never me
quick-span my body
bridge my sea
antipodes' my camouflage
for you and me

we heave
and mark off the night
but in the morning
you disappear from sight

Disclosure, III

should I melt
beyond all prissy constraint
rise to Orinoco cresting
hard on to vulve and valve

I have a question
before I spurt prisms for you
come all creamy and new to the world

have you really looked in my eyes
seen the nakedness seen the fear
have you seen your perfect image there

if in your face
there is no haunt
to kiss my sear
we'll roll
but you'll not have me here

Disclosure, IV

when Orincoco dried
I cried and felt the steamy lull
before all cracking broke loose

alluvial bent to sere
and withered birds to fluff
no jaws were satisfied

here is the place of dry crawling things
here is where my love lay down
where once a mighty river flowed

seek me not

Disclosure, V (Grandmother)

unless you dug her grave
and sucked her bones
you'll never know me

how can you hear her cries at night
and fathom the shape of my ear

her hand was a map
of unknown place
it rubbed my fevered brow
and gave me geography

can you travel there

hers was a voice
that never was
blowing through her bones
can make her new
but never true
I sing to that voice

yield all your mastery
only the dead are supreme

Dwelling In

fast-holding
is a life in depth and dark
when liberties are narrow

light's razor executes
no health confers
the game is waiting
wasting
withholding breath

the dark creates its creatures
and if the light relent
what might emerge
bears no telling
no telling

More Than All

the jungle mumble
has its own chorus
which ear can't hear

fast dark
is like a curtain
after which
no lights appear

instead a rumble
of no conduct
myriad solo
to no point
make ear a guise
for hearing
and harmony
hearing's further wall

Passing Through

when large birds squawk and swoop
no downy time is here
but ceremonies of another kind

fix mud
and rake the leavings
set the sun
and line the river bank

let each his march
proceed
survey perimeter
and enter into night

interior's cauldron
sinks all sound
but leaves sufficient sign
to where we're bound

duty-bowed and grieved
of all our days

Apostrophe

let us slide to the sucky mud
where other creatures wait

be bait to scaly slither
when they beckon hither

recognize that size
of horror's face
is but a measure
of our pace

our centaur's tread
is firmed by dread
we march where others stick
never looking when they're sick

o firmament
bastion of our ease
remove the shine
from our disease
help us plod
to other gods
remove the eye
that lets us die
so monstrously

On The Banks of Orinoco

the skin-bag babies on their knees
emit small squeak
and holders never speak
but stare

in both directions
draw a line
from in to out
and pluck dull music
steady as the flow
beneath them

time's lost measure
gives them fixity
broken only
by the pea-gurgle below
the dangle of bone
that once was flesh
of sitter's flesh
at home

Declaration

everybody fools everybody
for all language is a lie
and gesture lives in the losing

pale smell of life
sinks soundlessly into brain
decrepit movement
masks whatever pain
our glimpse allows

how then may I know you
what void make I mine
to penetrate your other
centrify our line

we have a chancy step
to grate for privilege
whenever is too late
but always
all we have
so speak

The Last Horizontal

the last horizontal
is where the birds at last alight
and preen in growing night
small clicks to mark the dark
as endless Orinoco flows

there will I squat and dimly watch
no movements that I care
the birds will lift a leg
and beady stare
non nuance in the park
that wears me in its mantle

coming down and coming in
I sleep and think of you

Flow On

who can say what Orinoco knows
its flow so silent and unseen

a razor line that skims its sheen
no shriek proclaims
no water maims

but cut though disappeared
runs deep
to where the Orinoco sleeps
nesting all our dreams
and all our pain

come voyage on her calm
billow in her breeze
though onward we propel
amid the banking green
and silent scream
we rest and know we rest
upon a seeming
that is all we are
and has its end
in Orinoco's flow

Down Farm

I seek a holiday
for dismembered thought
like so many wingless birds
stumbling in the dust

their croak
will be my new music
and dust in mouth
I'll sing and choke
gagging on a foul ecstasy

what a band we'll be
mutants of the word
thoughts never heard

but alive
in our barnyard
by the chopper's axe

Procession

when dry rattling
passes for laughter
a special time has come

for crippled birds
featherless and scorched
crawling white toads
and proud pests

hoarse parade
behind we follow
stump-throated
and coated with a sticky glaze

marching
sweat-occluded
into yellow haze
we are the proud humps
of latter-day
sickly ingluing
vestigial of an age

Proposal

enfold all my vanities
lest I be too naked
mark my flesh
with naked stare

I am aware
if only dim
the loveliness
of what I am

spent of my seeming
I would rot
and this foul creature
be your lot

love me
of my choosing
for should you win
you would be losing

Statement

each moment dies
and then becomes
a larger entity

engulfing all
into a one

we lie
upon an immensity
ignorant and swift
to no purpose

yet a death occurs

Warning, I

the birds are but one face
of whatever we've always known

beak-strewn
and beady-eyed
of thousand song

within/beyond
a heart beats strong
love what you cannot know
know what you cannot love
beware the peck
that pokes an eye

blindness
is a commission in darkness

Warning, II

if I should shed my skin
would you rub the rawness
kiss it clean with love

would you display
an array of organ
pulsing naked
tissue to the world

and say
this is my only love
bleeding as he is

I warn you
take my clothes
and this is what I am

Lecture, I

intransigencies crack my bones
remote as they may seem
from royal cause

and who would be the fool
to name them
when no surface needs
to tame them

I glide smoothly in your life
at show in every sunlight
for the exigencies of life

but none the less
I cripple
clip foundation's bones
in arcane fight

and who to say
what blood to shed
or show the course
we choose to dead

loving is or should
be vast suspicion
of good cause

Lecture, II

as much as any remnant
represents me
casts a shadow
on my life
bespeak me you
and tell the world
that I exist

and no foul claim is this
I give you
for the balance of my life
no scale can weigh
I am all odd proportion
and require of you
a certain sacrament
by force of will
investment
of your charm
to prove your passion

what else is love
but this odd requite
something given
in despite

Confidence

with words
do I create this sentience
above all quirky chemistry
and photos of the mind

I could not fully love you
did I not articulate
weave into this form
my arcane longing

mute encounter
passion's writhing
does not suffice
does not indite
this time's new notch

so bear with me
let me
now and then compose
while you repose

and when you wake
more gladly
will I make
all manner of disruption

Mouth, I

the mouth has no control
in certain situations

minutest gape
and faintest quiver
are all articulation

screaming in mute sign
that all design
is but a serving
to sudden masters of the flesh

o you knowers
of invisibilities
does your wisdom ever descend
to confirming touch

What Walls Enclose

no museum can contain
life's passing
until every apple
rolls like a head

we see on every wall
a moment's fall
and then a frame

life there
is all the same
the tension leaves the room
to ghosts
as we emerge
chrysalis to the new

Mouth, II

what spits out speech
consumes
contains a void

what armature of our passage
incorporates our lies
and gives invisibility
cheap clothing

what grinds up substance
into constituencies
of mean resolve
and sudden power

let us not name this thing
let us merely wonder
let us keep it at rest
if only for a moment

Tongue

the tongue can quickly dart
like peeping bird from nest
or tongue can grossly fill the mouth
be softly choking flesh
at its furthest extent
it can wriggle forthrightly
or be saucy as a new shoot
lewdly lick
give evidence of lubrication
for all our fitful starts
or jackhammer conclusion

how then contain
this coated realm
so pussy-sheathed
and arrogant

tongue is both constituency
and domain

Random Thought

does anyone know
or care
how many teeth in a mouse's mouth

waiting for trains is never dull
the mice dart in and out
feeding on residue
of a certain largesse

if my liver twitched
I'd never know it
just maybe die

I'd say the teeth and twitch
have some connection
unholier than I can say
but holier than I am

Provision

a certain studied stupidness
is best for most occasions
best mask
for other's front
and becoming modesty

life gives us opportunity
something other
gives us grace
to make a space between
be little seen
and little seem

Fly

who isn't a fly
particularly stuck on paper

stuck flies have their society
and tolerate disgrace
gender race

the realm of the sticky
provokes buzzing chorus
vast pantomime
of ideal life

crawling as our others see us
who would be so rash to free us

Dreamer

I dreamed a worm crawled in my left nostril
—what kind of dream is that
what kind of dream is any dream

I am the traveling creature
and I dream myself
dream myself dreaming
to right some balance
set some score

o worm
would that I could tell your logic
feel your way
so I could wake and see my dream
you are the beam of
rise from this sleep
I call life
and die

Manifesto

here is a theater a mirror a world
behold me in reflect
I am the stuff you're stuck on
better or worse

we thieve our action
and back to glass
relieve ourselves
confident as squirrels

back me into time
coordinate of endless rhyme
to no repose
I am the figure of no image